best Halloween candy ever—
before it got stale

best Valentine ever—
not counting chocolate ones!

Amelia's Best Year Ever

Favorite Amelia Stories from American Girl Magazine

by Marissa Moss

(and notebook-expert Amelia)

best New Year's confetti ever

best summer sand castle ever — before the waves hit it

best make-a-wish dandelion ever — the wish came true!

American Girl®

Baby New Year

Old Man Old Year

TWEET!!
HAPPY NEW YEAR!

This notebook is dedicated to
Elise Primavera—
may you have your best year ever!

yearbook

book of the
year!

Pleasant Company Publications
8400 Fairway Place
Middleton, Wisconsin 53562

Book design by Amelia

Cataloging-in-Publication data available from the Library of Congress

First Pleasant Company Publications printing, 2003
An Amelia® Book

Gobble,
gobble.

American Girl magazine is published by
Pleasant Company Publications. For subcription information
ask a parent to call 1-800-234-1278.

BOO!
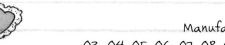

Manufactured in China.
03 04 05 06 07 08 09 LEO 10 9 8 7 6 5 4 3 2 1

where am
I?

When am I? Is
it February yet?

You never know how a day is going to turn out.
Some days you wish you'd never gotten out of bed.
Some days you feel like you're walking on air. And
some days are in-between.

I'm light as a feather!

Ho, hum.

YAWN!

Groan!

I'm going to keep a notebook for a year, collect a bunch of days, and see what I end up with. I'm hoping that if I look at a whole year of writing, there'll be more good stuff than bad.

The Scale of Days — Good or Bad, Which Side Is Heavier?

Oof, they're both weighty.

I can't keep my arms up like this for long.

Good things go here. ↘

Bad things go here. ↙

ice cream, presents, prizes, cool experiments, fun stuff

broken promises and toys, hurt feelings and skinned knees, barf bags and bad grades

Cleo's smelly socks

WHAT I LOVE ABOUT FALL

fresh, new school supplies ↓

Pink Pearl®

↑ This eraser will never be this Pink again.

making acorn people ↑

↑ colorful leaves on my favorite tree

↑ pumpkins, jack-o-lanterns, and pumpkin pie

trick-or-treating

crisp autumn air ↓

I'm not sure how to draw it, but I know what I mean.

Wheee!

↑ jumping into piles of leaves

Cleo as a pirate ↑

BAD THINGS ABOUT FALL

BRRRINNG!

waking up early for school

raking leaves and cleaning gutters

Bleh!

eating too much Halloween candy

Mom dressing up for Halloween

Don't I make a good bride of Frankenstein?

How embarrassing!

confusing school schedules

Hmmm, if it's Tuesday, history comes first...

...unless it's the second week of the month...

...then P.E. would come first...

...or would it?

Thanksgiving leftovers

It's the third day in a row of turkey sandwiches for lunch — bleh!

homework again

SCHOOL STORIES

Sept. 18

The best part of starting school is getting new supplies. The worst part is getting new clothes and seeing how much I haven't grown since last year. It never fails — I'm always the smallest kid in the class. Mom says I'm getting big, but she's a mom — she has to say that.

next-shortest kid, relieved to have someone even shorter

me

tallest kid, able to reach the highest books, see movies without being blocked, and never be bumped into by grown-ups who don't notice her existence

Will I always be looking up people's noses instead of face-to-face?

Sept. 20

My teacher, Ms. Busby, announced today that since we're fifth graders, we have a responsibility to help the younger kids. Some students are going to monitor the playground, and some will help in the library. But I've got a special job — I get to tell stories to the kindergartners every Friday for 15 minutes.

You can use a felt board and cut some felt into animals and people to help tell your stories.

Sounds great!

I was excited! I remember going to the library when I was little and listening to stories told that way.

Things you do in kindergarten but never again: →

eat Play-doh and paste ↓

Yum! My favorite flavor!

sing "I'm a Little Teapot" ↓

Sept. 28

Today was my first day telling stories. I was really nervous! But when I got there, the classroom looked so cozy and familiar. It even smelled familiar — that old crayon-and-glue smell. All the kindergartners sat cross-legged on the rug, looking up at me and just waiting for me to talk.

get your name on a who-lost-a-tooth chart ↓

It usually looks like a giant tooth or has a tooth-fairy wand on it

↑

make a plaster handprint— to be "treasured forever"?

I sat in one of those baby-sized chairs. I just fit— barely. →

They were so cute and tiny! Was I ever that small? Suddenly I felt huge! ↓

My voice was kind of squeaky at first, but then my story got going, and I forgot to be nervous. I came to a SCARY part and their eyes all got big. When I made something silly happen, they laughed. I had so much fun! Now I can't wait to do it again.

I guess I've grown after all. Maybe I'm still short next to the other fifth graders, but with the kindergartners, I'm definitely the biggest kid in the class!

The End

SCARED STIFF

Things to really be afraid of:

um, um...

↑
giving oral reports in front of the class

October 25

Carly <u>really</u> wants to go to this haunted house by our school. I told her it's a waste of time. Who's scared of peeled grapes and cold spaghetti? Not me!

Want to touch some "eyeballs"??
really grapes ↑

← Just Jell-O (take a taste!)

Feel the "guts"!
← cold, cooked spaghetti

"Innards," anyone? ↑

October 27

Carly insists it's <u>fun</u> to be scared, and she promises that the haunted house <u>will</u> be scary. So I said I'd go, but I'm only going to be a good friend. I know it'll be <u>so</u> predictable!

Open wide!

↑
the dentist

October 29

Just like I thought, the haunted house started out with the usual grapes, Jell-O and spaghetti.

My little pooky-ooky!

↑
relatives who pinch your cheeks and hug too tight

← lots of cobwebs and rubber spiders – of course!

In the second room, a ghost and a skeleton leaped out at us. Carly grabbed my hand and asked if I was scared. "No way!" I said.

only rubber, not real! →
←

The next room was darker, and all we could see were some monster masks wailing and groaning. "Pretty scary, huh?" Carly hissed in my ear. "They're supposed to be scary," I said. "But you know they're just rubber."

↳ The haunted house was built in somebody's garage.

more truly
fearsome
frights ↓

↑ having your taco drip all over your shirt so you go to class with a big stain

OOOOO!

skull with glowing eye sockets →

A mummy moaned at us in the third room, and a black cat screeched. I have to admit, it was a little creepy. The cat screech gave me some goose bumps, even.

rubber rat →

I bet it's paint on balloons, and when someone blows them up, they seem to magically appear. ↓

Then these glow-in-the-dark faces appeared out of nowhere, and there were eerie shrieks and moans.
"Now are you scared?" Carly whispered.
"It's a trick," I whispered back. But still . . .

The bench was wet — honest!

↑ getting a suspicious wet spot on your pants

The last room was so dark, I couldn't even see the way out. At first it was dead quiet. We didn't know what to look for or where to go. Then out of nowhere, we heard the **ROAR** of a chain saw! And a horrible, horrible laugh!

I practically yanked Carly's arm off. I pulled her with one hand while I groped for the exit with the other. The saw was getting closer, my heart was pounding faster, and then there was the exit and we just flew out of there!

Carly looked at me.
"So were you scared?"
"**YES!**"

Bye!

SCHOOL BUS

↑ missing the bus

I felt like my hair was standing straight up. →

Carly said I looked like I'd seen a ghost — I was afraid I'd become a ghost!

I said. Now that my heart was beating normally and my goose bumps were gone, I could say that. Carly was right — it was scary. Tomorrow we take Cleo. ★

Poor Max is the turnip. ↓

Max's face when he heard his role ↑

Monday, November 7

I wanted to be a Pilgrim. Or a Native American. But when Ms. Busby gave out parts for the Thanksgiving play, I got stuck with Corn. An ear of corn! What kind of part is that? The only thing worse is the turkey. Or the turnip.

Being corn reminds me of kindergarten when we did a play on the food pyramid and no one wanted to be Fats. Guess who got the part? I seem to have horrible luck when it comes to school plays.

Hooray!!

↑ Maya is a Pilgrim.

I wore a long cardboard box painted yellow and a yellow swim cap so I'd look like a stick of butter — how adorable!

← Nadia was Bread. She said it was good that I was Fats because we went together like Bread and Butter. (But she wouldn't trade my Butter for her Bread.)

Not the turkey, pleeeze!

↑ Sorry, Jacqueline — you are the turkey!

Tuesday, November 8

Carly came over after school so we could practice the play together. She gets to be a Native American and her mom is making a beautiful dress with beads on it for her. She is _so_ lucky! I don't have any ideas yet for my costume. Maybe I should glue popcorn on a green garbage bag and just cut a hole for my head.

Susie is a Native American. ↓

Saturday, November 19

fashion statement of the year →

I have to admit, I'm getting good at this corn stuff. I've memorized my speech about how Native Americans taught

Thank you, thank you!

Carly gets to wear beautiful moccasins. ↘

I've been working on a corny accent, but so far I just sound silly. ↙

the Pilgrims to grow corn, but I need something to give this part

PIZZAZZ!

Sunday, November 20

It's a good thing Mom made me clean my room today. I was just about to throw away a bag of old Halloween candy when I got a GREAT idea that will make Corn not so corny. Now I've just got to come up with a good costume.

I know just how to use this ancient candy corn! ↙

What does corn sound like, anyway? Yellow, buttery, salty — but how do you get that in a voice?

Tuesday, November 22

Hooray!!! THREE CHEERS for my corn costume. I finished it just in time for the performance. It turned out TERRIFIC!

Everyone cheered when I threw the candy corn (they didn't care that it was stale). Ms. Busby said I was the best corn she'd ever seen. The whole play went well— except when the turnip tripped on the turkey and fell flat on his face. (Max was like a mashed turnip.) Mom said I was a-maize-ing! ★

mmmm, good! ↓

What did one ear of corn say to the other?

I dunno, what?

Meet ya at the corner! Corn-er, get it?

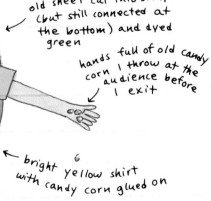

This part of the sheet is left white.

old sheet cut into strips (but still connected at the bottom) and dyed green

hands full of old candy corn I throw at the audience before I exit

← bright yellow shirt with candy corn glued on

← green leggings

← even green socks, shoes, and shoelaces!

WHAT I LOVE ABOUT WINTER

delicate snowflakes

presents, of course!

ice looks like doilies

silvery branches on my favorite tree

BE MINE
O U KID
LET'S GO

making sentences out of candy hearts

SWEET
4 U!
HONEY BUN

a steaming mug of hot chocolate with an avalanche of marshmallows

curling up with a good book on a cold, gray day

making snow creatures

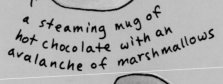

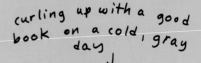

toe socks — they're like gloves for your feet!

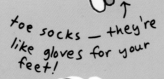

blowing puffs of air that you can see

BAD THINGS ABOUT WINTER

chattering teeth

writing thank-you notes for presents

Achoo!

getting sick

icicles dripping from your nose

galoshes

Help! I'm being eaten by a jacket!

bulky coats

shoveling snow

being stuck inside day after day

Lemme outta here!

TERRIBLE TWOS

Help!

sweet, innocent eyes

Mom says ice cream is a very nutritious dinner.

↑
me, six years old
↓

I go to bed at 8:00, but I can read as long as I like.

I always sit this close to the TV.

December 1

I want to babysit, but Mom thinks I'm too young. But I took care of my half brother George when I visited Dad last summer. Besides, I should be an EXPERT because I remember all the tricks I played on _my_ sitters when I was little.

George was cute → until he → exploded!

December 3

I didn't convince Mom I could babysit, but she did agree I could be a mother's helper. That means I help with kids while the mom's at home but busy with other stuff. I won't get paid as much, but I won't have to change diapers either. (Phew!)

December 5

I got my first job! Ms. Hua is giving a holiday party, and she needs me to take care of her twins while she gets ready and during the party.

They're three years old and VERY cute!

← They're not identical twins, so it's easy to tell them apart.

Holly

Ivy →

December 8

I'm all set for the twins. Here's what I'm bringing:

All-Purpose Mother's-Helper Kit

my old stuffed bear— for extra-strength cuddling →

sidewalk chalk — something to draw with that washes off, for nontoxic fun

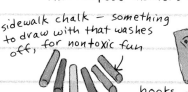

books — some of my old favorites, for fast-acting relief

animal crackers— we can play with them if we don't eat them for emergency hunger
↓

books hidden in the dishwasher (Always check before turning on to avoid soggy pages!)

↑ surprises under their pillows (Oh, that's where the peanut butter sandwich went!)

rubber ducky ↓

↑ strange items placed in my shoe (Plastic toys are O.K., but snails are NOT!)

WARNING: Small children may be hazardous to your peace (and piece) of mind!

They'll calm down as soon as you play with them. They just want attention.

Or read to them. They love books.

December 10

The party was today. Even before I got to the house, I could hear the twins screaming—definitely not a good sign. Ms. Hua was REALLY glad to see me. She was right, the twins did love books — scribbling on, tearing, and stomping on them! Instead of cuddling my bear, they threw him in the trash (at least they missed the toilet!). I promised them animal crackers if they were good, but they just grabbed the crackers and got crumbs everywhere. I didn't know what to do, and the guests would be coming soon!

fierce wild animals →

GRRR!

← or toddlers—you pick!

ROAR!

I was afraid the girls would start throwing the party food next, so we went outside. (It is VERY hard to get flailing arms into coat sleeves!) I took out the only part of my kit they hadn't ruined yet and started to draw.

It was a holiday party, so I drew holiday stuff on the front walk. ↓

Holly colored this. ↙

← Ivy colored this.

Since there was no snow, we drew snowmen. ↗

The twins loved it, and they wanted to draw, too! Some of their scribbles were pretty good! When the guests came, they loved our decorations. Best of all, the girls were so tired, they were little angels the rest of the night. All I had to do was read Curious George 62 times. Oh well, the next time I take care of them, I'll know it by heart. ★

a Very Special Delivery

December 13

   I've been thinking of what I should send my pen pal, Mako, for Christmas. I haven't seen him since we met at the Grand Canyon last summer, but he's already written me 6 letters. He even sent me a picture of his house in Japan. I've sent him pictures back, but now I want to give him something special, something American that he can't get in Japan.

← Mako's school photo — he looks just like I remember

(left margin, rotated) Mako says his family hangs stockings by the bathtub pipe since they don't have a chimney.

December 14

   My sister, Cleo, says how do I know Mako is Christian — maybe he doesn't celebrate Christmas. O.K, maybe he doesn't, but I can always call it a New Year's present. Only what if Japanese New Year isn't January 1st? Does it really matter? I love getting presents ANY time of year.

← stockings hung by bathtub with care

Inside the box were candles — they look like fruit snacks, but they're way too pretty to eat.

December 15

   Mako celebrates Christmas <u>and</u> Japanese holidays. Before I could send him anything, <u>he</u> sent <u>me</u> a Christmas present. It's a beautiful box made from special washi paper. Mako made it himself!

someone taking a bath

← Japanese bathtub (I imagine)

Mako sent a photo of his sister, Yumi, dressed up for a holiday last November called Shichi-go-san (that means "7,5,3" because the holiday is just for kids those ages). It's like an extra birthday. ↘

December 17

Mako's descriptions of his holidays make me want to go to Japan and see for myself. I want to write interesting things back, but I don't know what. And I still don't know what to give him.

I mean, this is really dressed up. It took Yumi 2 hours just to put on her makeup and get her hair ready!

Wow— talk about high heels!

The bow at the back was so heavy, Yumi almost fell backward!

I copied the recipe for doughnuts from Mom's cookbook and put it in Mako's notebook. ↘

December 18

It's almost Christmas and I still haven't gotten Mako's present. I wish I could make him something cool. I don't even have beautiful candy to send. Everything here is so ordinary!

↑ *I wonder if Japanese notebooks have splotchy covers. I bet not.*

jelly beans are kind of pretty, but are they special enough? →

I like how they look, but hate how they taste ↗

December 19

I got another letter from Mako—already! He was so excited, he had to write me about a new doughnut store. He'd never tasted a doughnut before! I would never think a doughnut is special, but I guess it all depends on what you're used to.

← Doughnuts are another thing that look better than they taste.

You can win prizes when you buy a doughnut—Mako sent me one of his.

Doughnut Song:
"Oh, I ran around the corner, and I ran around the block, and I ran right into a doughnut shop, and I picked up a doughnut, and I wiped off the grease, and I handed the lady a five-cent piece. Well, she looked at the nickel, and she looked at me, and she said, 'This nickel's no good to me. There's a hole in the middle and it goes right through.' And I said, 'There's a hole in the doughnut, too.' Thanks for the doughnut. Bye now!"

December 20

I finally found the PERFECT thing for Mako—it's a notebook, American style, with a set of colored pencils and a bunch of neat erasers. I got the idea from the doughnuts. I mean, even the most ordinary stuff is different— and cool—when it's from another country. Maybe Mako will send me a Japanese notebook someday. I'd love that! ★

Love, Who?

February 14

When I put my hand in my jacket pocket at lunch, I found something in it — a pink envelope and a bag of candy!

When I was little, Valentine's Day was so much fun! It meant getting lots of candy ↓

and lots of cards, ↓

Little glitter hearts fell out of the card. ↓

a surprise in my pocket ↓

Roses are red, Violets are blue, Ice cream is cool, and so are you! ♡MAX♡

A little bag of chocolate hearts was tucked in there, too. ↓

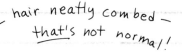

and it didn't matter who gave them to you. Now it's not so simple. You don't give cards to everyone in your class. Now it means something when you give a valentine — and when you get one!

A valentine from Max! I like Max, but I don't <u>like</u> like him. It's nice to get a card, and it's definitely nice to get chocolate, but <u>now</u> what am I supposed to do? I don't want to hurt his feelings. I just don't think of him that way. I mean, I don't think of <u>anyone</u> that way, but <u>especially</u> not him!

Max looked goony and lovesick all day. I couldn't bear to face him.

hair neatly combed — that's not <u>normal</u>!

stars in his eyes — what's he seeing, anyway?

When I see Max, I remember the time he laughed so hard, milk shot out of his nose.

Normally he looks excited and energetic — I like him better that way.

heart thumping wildly

Maybe I can send Max a message with those candy hearts.

O U KID   U R SWEET   BUT   I LIKE U   NOT.

valentine types we know and ♡:
↓

Actually, the hearts sound a little mean. I'd do better telling him myself.

February 15

Today Max kept looking at me like I'd suddenly grown an extra head or something. Carly said I've got to talk to him, but I can't even look him in the eye. How do I tell him thanks, but no thanks?

↑ frilly, lacy kind (usually from an aunt or a grandma)

Those cardboard cupids Ms. Busby put up in the classroom keep reminding me how Max must feel — like he's got an arrow in his heart.
How can I hurt his feelings?

What do naked, winged babies have to do with love anyway? They should at least wear diapers!

↑ superhero kind (what does fighting crime have to do with liking someone?)

February 16

This morning Max was staring at me like something was smudged on my face. That was enough! I decided I had to talk to him. Before I could change my mind, I went up to him, and his face turned bright red. Yikes! It was going to be even worse than I'd imagined. Luckily, he started talking first.

You're the beary best!
↑ cute, big-eyed animal kind (for people you like but don't like like)

Then Max looked at the floor and not at me at all!

cheeks burning pinker than the valentine

Um, uh, Amelia, um... ya know that card you got from me, that valentine? Um, I don't know how to say this, but I put it in the wrong jacket. I mean, I like you, but I don't like like you. The card was really for Charisse... I'm sorry.

That's O.K. — I'm not mad or anything, but I did eat the candy.

Boy, did I feel relieved!

So it all turned out O.K., except Charisse didn't get her valentine. Now she'll have to wait till next year. I wonder if I'll get a valentine then — a real one, not a mistake. Maybe a mistake is better — you don't have to worry about liking the person... and you still get to eat the chocolate. ★

↑ homemade, scrawled-on paper hearts (the kind only a mom — or dad — could love)

BAD THINGS ABOUT SPRING

SCIENTIFIC DISCOVERY

March 15

The science fair is in two weeks, and I can't wait! I love doing experiments—you get to make cool things happen, not just listen while someone explains things to you. I want to do something __interesting__.

me as a mad scientist →

straaaange concoction

← wild hair from experiment with static electricity

safety goggles in case of escaped electrons

smelly potion—DO NOT DRINK!

things you always see at science fairs

↑ the baking soda-vinegar volcano

crumb of cheese

↑ the pet mouse in a maze

no sun   sun
↓   ↓

the plant-growing experiment

scientific sugar-water solution

someone always grows sugar crystals

March 17

Shopping at the store with Mom today gave me an idea. She was complaining about how the last time she bought bread, it went moldy right away. I'm going to do a project on how different breads grow mold.

March 18

I bought ❸ kinds of bread — a sourdough baguette wrapped in just a paper bag instead of plastic, a whole wheat good-for-you kind of bread, and Fluff-O white bread, my favorite.

→ bread snowman with poppy-seed face

Fluff-O is also good for bread sculpture — you can wad it into any shape! →

vrooom! a bread car!

MY HYPOTHESIS

The baguette will have the most mold since it's already been left in the air.

The wheat will grow dark moldy spots.

happy mold face

The white will have white fluffy mold.

Last year, Cleo blindfolded kids and had them eat red M&Ms, then green ones, then yellow, then brown. The amazing scientific conclusion: they taste the same! (But the point was that Cleo got to eat a lot of candy.)

more brick than bread

The baguette is hard as a rock, but <u>no</u> mold!

↑ The whole wheat has patches of green and white fuzz.

The white bread looks the same as ever— <u>no</u> mold! ↖

Now I really <u>am</u> a mad scientist— mad at this bread for being so unscientific!

there's always a tornado-in-a-bottle ↘

↑ two soda bottles filled with water and taped together— swirl around to create a whirlpool

March 27

This is a disaster! The science fair is in three more days and nothing's happening the way it's supposed to. Help! Only one bread is growing mold! What went wrong?

March 28

Cleo almost made a sandwich with my bread. She asked what was I trying to do — ruin her appetite? I told her to keep her hands (and teeth!) off my science project, even if it FLOPPED. She said, "Maybe it's not what you expected, but it's <u>still</u> an experiment." Thanks a lot, Cleo! Maybe it's not too late to test if people can taste the difference between pink and blue gum balls.

↑ something with a light bulb

March 29

I read the wrappers the bread came in, and they gave me an idea. Cleo was actually right. I just have to think about what happened, not what I <u>wanted</u> to have happen.

it's only good for a clay substitute! I don't eat Fluff-O anymore—

model of the solar system— also a mobile

March 30

a happy scientist ↘

HOW PRESERVATIVES AFFECT MOLD GROWTH

The baguette has no preservatives, so it turns rock hard in a day— too hard and dry for mold to grow.

The whole wheat bread has <u>some</u> preservatives, so it stays moist and encourages mold growth.

Fluff-O white bread is <u>so</u> full of preservatives that even though it's not dry, mold can't grow.

Cleo said I've <u>really</u> ruined her appetite now — she's not eating white bread again! I told her this is how the best discoveries are made — by accident! ★

Speech bubbles and labels in the illustration: "Not last night, but the night before", "jump for joy", "twenty-four robbers came knocking at my door", "← Carly", "← me", "Maya →"

Here are some awards I could win:

Best Hotel Soap Collection

Most carsick Sister

April 3

Our school is having a Double Dutch jump-rope contest and Carly, Maya, and I are entering it. I've tried writing and drawing contests, but this is the first time I've done anything like this. I'm terrible at sports, but Carly and Maya say we have a chance to win. They say it will be fun even if we don't win. But it won't be so fun if everyone ends up laughing at me.

April 10

clean white shoes with rainbow laces — they make me bounce higher

All this practicing is exhausting!

Jumping rope <u>used</u> to be fun.

Now it's work!

I love the minute right before you jump in, when the rhythm of the rope slap-slapping the pavement starts throbbing in your feet and then — jump! you're in!

↑ Longest Gum Wrapper Chain (longer than Nadia's)

April 13

The contest is not until next week and already I'm <u>so</u> nervous. At recess you can tell who's going to be in the contest. There are lots of kids jumping rope. And some of them are amazing — doing splits and flips, fancy stuff   like that. I'm just trying for a   →   good cartwheel.

↑ Best Nose Artist

But will I get a medal for jumping rope???

How does she do it? How do her pants do it?

Lucy takes ballet lessons, so a split is easy for her.

April 19

Tomorrow is the contest! I can't even get a cartwheel right and Carly can do a handspring. She deserves first prize even if I don't.

April 20

I have never been this NERVOUS in my life! My hands were so sweaty, I thought the jump rope would slip right out. When we started to chant, my voice was all squeaky and wobbly. But then I caught the rhythm of the rope from Maya, and I was O.K. Carly was perfect, like I knew she would be. Maya was great, too, with her extra-fast red hot peppers. Then it was my turn.

my stomach was queasy

my legs were spaghetti

the rainbow laces didn't help →

← my feet were lumpy meatballs

I listened to the smack of the rope, the beat of the rhyme, and suddenly my body knew what to do all by itself — even my cartwheel turned out O.K.

We didn't win a prize, but I felt like we'd won something anyway. Carly says next year we'll all be better. Maybe I'll even try a flip. ★

Mistakes I do NOT want to happen:

1.

tripping on the rope

2.

hitting my face on the rope when I jump in

3.

falling on my butt

4.

having my shoe fly off when I kick high

← Say it like "Chow!" No, not THAT kind of chow— it means "Hi!"

Ciao, Amelia!

Oodles of Noodle Doodles

April 23

Carly, Maya, and I joined the Italian Club at school because we thought it'd be fun to learn a foreign language and eat lots of pizza. So far we haven't eaten any pizza, but I'm learning some words.

when Ms. Tufarelli speaks Italian, it sounds so beautiful.

Buon giorno, ragazzi! Come state?*

*"Hello, kids! How are you?"

when I speak Italian, it sounds like gibberish.

I like-o speako Italiano. Uno piccolo biggolo something-O.*

* Adding an "O" doesn't make a word Italian, but it sounds better.

April 28

Italian is crazy! There are different words for "the" depending on whether the thing you're talking about is considered "masculine" or "feminine." But how can a factory be female and a book be male? Why is melon a boy, but pear a girl?

You can tell I'm a girl because I have eyelashes.

I see!

April 29

Ms. Tufarelli says that next week, we're going to an Italian restaurant. We'll have to read an Italian menu, order our food in Italian, and try to talk to each other only in Italian. (Our conversations will be very short!) Carly, Maya, and I are practicing all the food vocabulary we can think of.

il fegato (liver)

Words to be avoided:
i spinaci (spinach)

la melanzana (eggplant)

i ceci (beans)

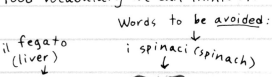

Pasta tasted better before I knew what the names meant.
↓

"Orecchiette" means little ears. (Dig in to those ears!)

"Farfalle" means butterflies. (Bow-tie noodles is more appetizing.)
↑

"Vermicelli" means little worms. (Yucch!)
↑

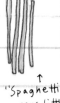

"Spaghetti" means little strings. (Tasty, eh?)
↑

"Linguine" means little tongues. (Blecch!)
↑

Handy-dandy Italian phrases:

"Per favore" (Pear fah-VOR-ay) means please.
"Grazie" (GRAH-tsyeh) means thank you.
"Delizioso" (DAY-lee-tsee-oh-zo) means yummy!

Pizza, per favore.

Grazie!

May 3

Well, yesterday we went to "Il Buon Forno" (The Good Oven), and it wasn't like when Ms. Tufarelli speaks Italian at all! The waiter spoke so quickly, he sounded like a tape on *FAST FORWARD*. The only words I understood were "Buona sera" (good evening). After that, I was lost! I did my best anyway and ordered a sandwich. The waiter burst out laughing, and Ms. Tufarelli explained I'd just asked for a diaper!

↑
Sandwich is "panino."

What I said was "pannolino."

↑
diaper— NOT edible!

My face was so red, I wanted to sink under the table! →

I just should have asked for spaghetti, but the only kind they had was made of spinach! At least I knew ~~that~~ word.

I wasn't the only one to make a mistake. For dessert Carly asked for "gelato al pesce," more words I knew.

When I told her she'd ordered <u>fish</u> ice cream, she couldn't stop laughing! She really wanted "gelato alla pe<u>sca</u>"— <u>peach</u> ice cream.

I had to laugh with her!

sardine sundae ↓

At least I knew what flavor I wanted—plain old chocolate. It sounds the same in both languages. Plus it's the one time you can add an "O" to an English word and get the  Italian one.

"gelato al chocolate-o" or "cioccolato"

Either way it's "delizioso!" ←

Is this what I ordered?

Even if I make some mistakes, learning Italian is fun. Who knows, maybe someday I'll meet an Italian girl and teach her to say "soup" instead of "soap!" ★

Spoonful of suds

Can't Make Up My Mind

The thing about makeup is it looks so tasty.

May 10

Today Cleo came home from her friend Gigi's house with a big bag of stuff. She wouldn't let me see what was in it, but I peeked while she was in the bathroom. At first I thought it was really old Halloween candy. Then I saw it was makeup. Mom says we can't wear makeup in public till we're older, but Cleo says she wants to practice. She's going to need a lot of practice.

I want to eat it more than I want to wear it.

WARNING: NOT EDIBLE
(not nutricious, not delicious!)

I watched Cleo put all this stuff on. I told her she looked like an alien. She told me I looked like a geek. Which is better-looking, a geek or an alien?

Cleo without makeup— eek, scary!

Cleo with makeup— froggy eyelids, cabbage lips, and a jelly-roll nose—too much!

May 12

Gigi came over today. She and Cleo locked themselves in the bathroom for <u>hours</u>. When they finally came out, they looked like an ad for how to wear makeup and how <u>NOT</u> to wear makeup. Cleo looked awful, but Gigi looked <u>great</u>. I wonder how <u>I</u> would look.

It all looks so cool in the cute little jars, but would it look cool on me?

Gigi—she looks beautiful no matter what

terrific earrings

beautiful fingernails

elegant eyes

sophisticated smile

graceful hands

eyeliner pencil– it's more fun to draw with it on paper than on my eyelids

hand before makeup

hand after makeup

Hello!

When I was little, I colored my nails with marker and I thought it looked great, but then I used to draw faces on my hands, too. Maybe makeup is better on my hands than on my face.

If I could name makeup here's what I'd call it:

May 15

Cleo was at Gigi's house today so I went into her room and tried on her makeup. (She won't notice if a tiny bit is gone.) I put aqua shock eye shadow on my eyelids and blueberry pie lipstick on my mouth and chocolate chip nail polish on my fingernails. When I was done, I looked like this:

boiled egg white

My eyelids felt itchy and slimy like a lizard licked them.

I tried for luscious lashes, but I got lumpy, clumpy lashes.

My lips felt slippery and that blueberry pie was not tasty.

Somehow these hands don't look elegant.

moldy algae green

stinky cheese yellow

the washcloth to hide the evidence

Washing all that gunk off wasn't easy – the washcloth was so caked with goo, I had to hide the evidence waaay at the bottom of the hamper.

I didn't look like an alien. I didn't look like a monster. I didn't look like a geek. But I didn't look like me, either. That was the worst part — I felt like it wasn't my face anymore. I couldn't wait to wash it off and be me again.

May 16

When I brushed my teeth this morning, I was glad to see my normal face in the mirror. Sometimes it's fun to dress up and wear masks and pretend to be someone else, but I wouldn't want to be like that all the time. I just want to stay me. ★

mud puddle brown

WHAT I LOVE ABOUT SUMMER

ice-cold lemonade

doing nothing under my favorite tree

cool, green shade

the ice cream truck— follow that tune!

grass tickling my bare feet

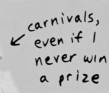

carnivals, even if I never win a prize

playing in the pool

sleeping as late as I want

summer fruit— watch out for sticky chins and fingers!

Whoa! Cannonball!

WHAT BUGS ME ABOUT SUMMER

YAAAAAA!

CARNIVAL THRILLS

June 5

My favorite part of June is when the carnival comes to town. Then I know summer's <u>really</u> started. Last night Mom took Carly and me. She said we could go wherever we wanted as long as we checked in with her by the cotton candy stand in an hour. We were free, free, FREE!

I wanted to play the boardwalk games and Carly wanted to go on rides, so we took turns. ↓

We went on the roller coaster first.

↑ You have to throw up your hands for the full effect.

The lights everywhere made it all so magical! ↓

WHEEL OF FORTUNE
FUN HOUSE
BUMPER CARS

During the day the same things look hokey, but at night they're beautiful. Even the air tasted better than daytime air.

It was hard to pick a game to play. I wanted to do <u>all</u> of them.

ringtoss ↗

balloon pop

PING!
shooting gallery ↗

I decided to try the ringtoss because I'm pretty good at horseshoes. One ticket got me three rings. And three rings got me a big fat ZERO! Ringtoss is <u>not</u> like horseshoes at all! Carly didn't even want to try — she said it wasn't worth it. So we went to get a snack instead. (It seemed safe since we'd <u>already</u> gone on the roller coaster.)

AIEEEEEE!

One of the things I love about carnivals is that there's nothing nutritious to eat — it's ALL junk food!

Don't look back down — that's always a mistake!

fried cheese ↓

fried dough ↓

fried fries ↓

And it all looks and smells exactly the same — like greasy batter.

But when we were walking around with our fries, I saw a little kid with a prize from the ringtoss booth. If that little kid could win, then I could, too. I just HAD to try again.

On my first ticket, a ring almost went over the bottle!

TING!

On my second ticket, the ring slipped off just as it was about to go over the bottle's neck — soooo close!

BOING!

On my third ticket, a ring actually went over the neck, but then bounced off!

KAHLUMP!

I thought I should win anyway — it was on for a second — but the guy said no.

Carly was getting mad at me. I'd already used up four tickets.

Carly is not the gambling type.

You're wasting money and time. Let's do something fun.

Please, please, pleeeeeease! Just once more.

She was right, but I was getting better. She gave me one last chance.

Finally I did it!

I WON!

TADA!

giant inflatable banana

How come the prizes look so good at the carnival and so crummy once they're in my room?

bug-eyed bear

ugly troll doll

I picked the banana — I don't know why.

which prize to pick? Which would I still want tomorrow?

stiff stuffed snake

Screaming as loud as you can is part of the ride.

Carly laughed and said, "What a hunk of junk. Was it worth five tickets?" The prize wasn't, but the feeling of winning — now that was definitely worth it!

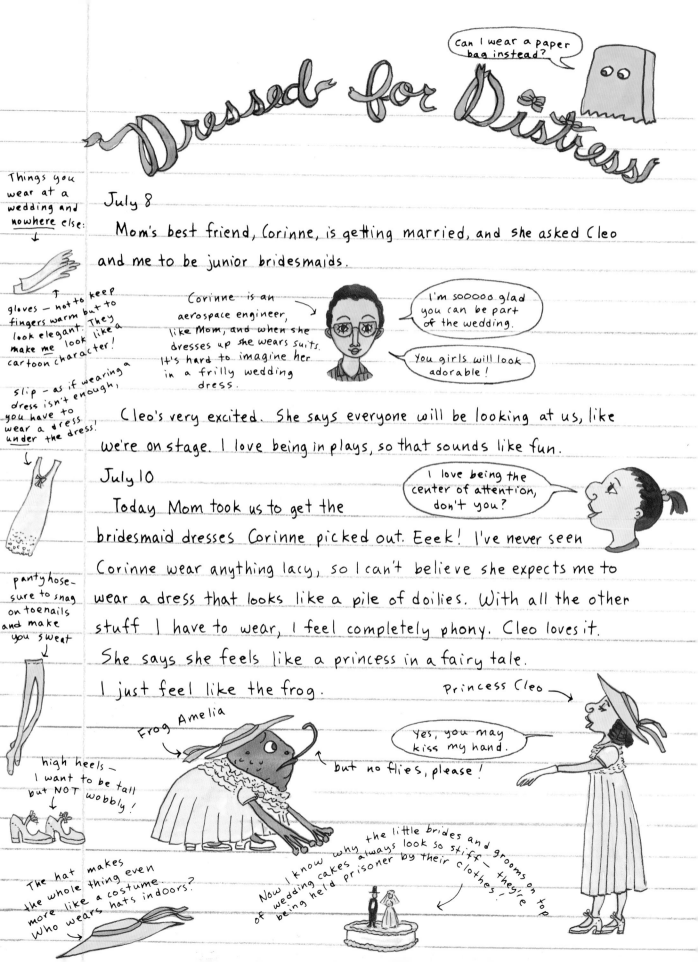

Dressed for Distress

Can I wear a paper bag instead?

July 8

Mom's best friend, Corinne, is getting married, and she asked Cleo and me to be junior bridesmaids.

Things you wear at a wedding and nowhere else:

gloves — not to keep fingers warm but to look elegant. They make me look like a cartoon character!

slip — as if wearing a dress isn't enough, you have to wear a dress under the dress!

pantyhose — sure to snag on toenails and make you sweat

high heels — I want to be tall but NOT wobbly!

Corinne is an aerospace engineer, like Mom, and when she dresses up she wears suits. It's hard to imagine her in a frilly wedding dress.

I'm sooooo glad you can be part of the wedding.

You girls will look adorable!

Cleo's very excited. She says everyone will be looking at us, like we're on stage. I love being in plays, so that sounds like fun.

July 10

Today Mom took us to get the bridesmaid dresses Corinne picked out. Eeek! I've never seen Corinne wear anything lacy, so I can't believe she expects me to wear a dress that looks like a pile of doilies. With all the other stuff I have to wear, I feel completely phony. Cleo loves it. She says she feels like a princess in a fairy tale.

I just feel like the frog.

I love being the center of attention, don't you?

Frog Amelia

Princess Cleo

Yes, you may kiss my hand.

but no flies, please!

The hat makes the whole thing even more like a costume. Who wears hats indoors?

Now I know why the little brides and grooms always look so stiff on top of wedding cakes — they're being held prisoner by their clothes.

Reasons why I don't want to be the center of attention:

What if I trip in my high heels?

What if I walk in the wrong direction? I didn't know I'd have to <u>rehearse</u> for this!

This way?

This way?

July 20

I had no idea being in a wedding could be such hard work! And just thinking about everyone staring at me as I walk down the aisle ALONE makes me feel as itchy as the dress does. I told Mom I couldn't go to the wedding tomorrow because I had a bad stomach ache. She said that was just nerves and I have to go.

What if I get the hiccups and can't hold them in?

July 30

I still felt like a lead ball was in my stomach—until we got to the church and I saw Corinne.

I'm so happy to have you here with me. You look like a princess!

She saw me looking at her and laughed.

I know this isn't the real me, but weddings are supposed to be like fairy tales. Thanks for being part of mine!

I thought she looked beautiful! And suddenly I felt like a princess, too! I didn't care if my neck itched or my fingers were sweaty. I was an important part of Corinne's very important day!

The wedding cake tasted like a sponge, but the candied violets were pretty.

I didn't feel like a frog anymore. I didn't trip in my high heels, and I only sweated a little bit. It was perfect! At the reception, Cleo and I took off our shoes, hats, and gloves, and we danced together. Dressing up was O.K., but dressing down was even better! ★

not champagne, but sparkling cider

clink!

You were a great bridesmaid!

So were you!

Dive On In!

Oops! I dripped on the page. I hope chlorine doesn't eat paper. ↑

Jumping Styles

Dead-Body Jump- Hold arms rigid at sides. Do not look down!

July 8

At the pool today it seemed like suddenly <u>all</u> the kids were using the high diving board, not the low one. Everyone but me. I like to dive, but the high dive is <u>so</u> high.

me on my towel, baking in the sun, safe on the ground →

sunscreen ↓

↑ Carly on the high dive— even standing she looks so graceful

July 9

When I saw Carly on the high dive, I really wanted to dive, too. She made it look so easy. By her third dive, I'd convinced myself I could do it, so I followed her up that loooong ladder.

I wanted to dive, but my feet didn't. They climbed back down the ladder. I told Carly I really had to go to the bathroom. (And I really did have to go — not to the bathroom, but down the ladder!)

Clown Jump- Hold nose, flail arm, and kick legs wildly.

July 11

There is a lot of stuff to do in a pool <u>besides</u> diving. Today I walked the whole way across the shallow end on my hands and chatted with Carly underwater (but all I heard was blubglublub).

We sounded like fish talking.

Cannonball- Curl up into a tight ball, and plunge in rear-first.

Why is a diving board so much like a stage? Just getting on it makes people notice you.

← Now when I see kids climbing the high dive and looking terrified, I know just how they feel.

Diving Styles
Cling-to-the-Board Dive—
Let go at the last minute and fall headfirst.

July 12

I'm not giving up on the high dive. This time I got all the way to the edge of the board. But somehow it was too scary to dive off headfirst. So I closed my eyes and JUMPED! It seemed like I fell forever, like parachuting without a chute. It was still scary, but FUN!

back up from my jump →

me dripping on the edge of the pool ←

Swimming Dive— Pretend to swim in the air – try not to land chin-first.

July 13

Yesterday's jump was as close as I've come to flying. Today I stood at the tip of the high dive, my toes poking off the edge and my hands together in front of my nose. I kept telling myself, "Do it, do it, do it," but I didn't do it. Then I stopped saying "do it" and my body just did it! I DOVE IN!

Belly-Flop Dive— to be avoided at all costs!

FROM THE HIGH DIVE!

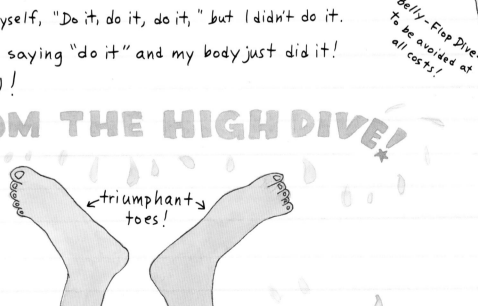

←triumphant→ toes!

FRIEND OR FOE?

Ways to get someone to notice you at a swimming pool:
↓

Do a LOUD belly flop!
↑

Torpedo out of the water as HIGH as you can.
↑

EEEK!

Wear a shark fin on your back.
↑

August 12

I was supposed to meet Carly at the pool today, but when I got there, she was already sitting with three other girls I didn't know. I'm never sure how to act around strangers, so I walked by hoping she'd notice me. But Carly was doubled over laughing and didn't even look up. So I just kept walking and jumped into the water.

I don't remember Carly ever laughing that hard at _my_ jokes.

They acted like they were best friends →

I thought Carly was _my_ best friend.

She hadn't even saved a place for me.
↑

I kept hoping Carly would see me in the water, but she didn't.

Blooop

sending thought waves underwater →

Carly, look in the pool, look in the pool!

Eventually, I turned into a prune and <u>had</u> to get out of the water. I didn't want to break into their little party, so I went and sat down by the snack bar. ALONE.

← No friend here.   Or here. →

How to tell friends from foes:

Hee hee!

Ha ha!

People who smile and laugh a lot are usually nice.

People who throw sharp objects are to be avoided.

I huddled on my towel like a useless lump.

I was trying not to be sad, but I felt invisible — like I wasn't as interesting to Carly as her new friends. And that made me stick to my towel like glue.

I stared at my toes as if they were fascinating.

Unfortunately, toes really aren't fascinating.

Have some popcorn.

People who share make good friends.

Finally Carly came to buy a drink and saw me. "Amelia," she said, "I wondered where you were! Didn't you see me over there? Come sit down and meet my cousins."

Cousins? Those girls were Carly's cousins? Not her new best friends?

All mine!

People who don't share should be left alone.

Hi!

Hi ya!

Howdy!

Ayesha

Taina

Zeena

How was I supposed to know? Carly didn't tell me her cousins were visiting from New York! It turned out they were really nice. And Zeena's even better at diving than Carly. She showed all of us some cool tricks, and I learned how to do a back dive. But the best part was, I made 3 new friends. ★

Hello.

Nice to meet you.

If someone is a friend of your friend, there must be something good about her. You might like her, too.

Bye, Amelia! Come see us in New York sometime!

I will!